DAVID GRANT

The Bet

Illustrated by Garry Parsons

BLOOMSBURY

LONDON OXFORD NEW YORK NEW DELHI SYDNEY

CONTENTS

Chapter One
The bet

Ed and Zac were sitting in class. Their teacher was handing out letters to everyone.

Ed stuffed his letter into his bag. He never read letters from school.

Zac read the letter quickly. His mum had got cross with him when she found about twenty letters from school, at the bottom of his bag. Now he made sure he read letters from school and showed his mum the important ones. This letter was definitely an important one.

"Wow!" said Zac. "A skiing and snowboarding weekend in Scotland! I definitely want to go on that."

"Snowboarding?" said Ed. He sounded excited too. "I'd love to go snowboarding!"

They were still talking about it as they walked home.

On the way they met Becca and Kat who were coming out of the corner shop.

"Did you get the letter about the trip?" asked Ed.

"Yes," said Becca. "There is no way I can go on that. It's really expensive. It costs two hundred pounds."

"Two hundred pounds?" said Zac. He hadn't

read that bit of the letter.

"I don't think my parents will pay that much," said Ed. He looked really disappointed.

In fact, all four of them looked disappointed.

"It's not fair," sighed Zac. "Only the rich kids will get to go snowboarding. And we get stuck here."

"Hey, maybe we could earn the money ourselves," cried Kat excitedly.

"Good idea!" said Ed. "I bet Zac and I could earn it easily."

"You and Zac?" said Becca. "We could earn way more than you two!"

"Bet you!" said Zac.

And that was how it all started.

Chapter Two
The boys

That night, Ed sent a text to Zac. He wrote,

> We need to win that bet and make more money than the girls. Any ideas?

Zac sent a text back.

> No.

But then, a few minutes later, Zac had an idea. He asked his mum about it and then sent another message.

> My mum says she will give us a fiver if we clean the house for her.

And that gave Ed an idea.

> We could go around all the houses on the estate. We could knock on doors and ask people if they want their house cleaned.

Zac wrote,

Brilliant idea!

My mum says we can borrow the proper vacuum cleaner she has for her cleaning job if we clean my house for nothing.

And she will show me how to use it.

Ed replied,

Cool! Come round on Saturday morning with the vacuum cleaner. We are definitely going to win that bet. Snowboarding, here we come!

Chapter Three
The girls

At exactly the same time as Ed and Zac were texting, Becca was texting Kat.

Becca wrote,

We need to win that bet and make more money than the boys. Any ideas?

Kat sent a text back.

Loads. We could bake cakes and sell them at school. We could get all the rubbish out of my dad's shed and sell it at a car boot sale. We could sell all my old toys on the internet.

Becca wrote,

My mum says she will give us a fiver if we clean her car.

That gave Kat another idea.

We could clean lots of people's cars. We could go round all the houses on the estate. We could knock on doors and ask people if they want their cars cleaned.

Becca wrote,

Brilliant idea!

We can borrow the bucket and sponge my dad uses to clean his car. And he has a great big bottle of car shampoo.

Kat replied,

Cool! Bring it all round on Saturday
morning. We will make loads of money. We
are definitely going to beat the boys!

Becca sent a text to Ed.

We are going to wash cars on Saturday.
We should make loads of money and win
the bet.

"Don't be so sure about that," said Ed.

Chapter Four
Let the games begin

At eleven o'clock on Saturday morning, Zac and Ed came out of Zac's house.

Ed's phone buzzed.

He got it out of his pocket. There was a text from Kat. It said,

Only been going two hours and made thirty quid already. How about you?

"Why don't we start on Elm Road?" said Ed.

They set off up the road. Ed was carrying a mop, and a bucket full of bottles and tins of cleaning stuff. Zac brought the vacuum cleaner. He pulled it along by the hose. It rolled along behind him on its wheels, like a dog on a lead.

"This is really embarrassing," said Zac. "Can't we make money some other way? I hate cleaning."

"Everyone hates cleaning," said Ed. "People will be happy for us to do it for them. Soon they will be throwing money at us!"

They arrived at the front gate of the first house on Elm Road.

Ed walked up to the front door and knocked.

An old man opened the door a little way. He was bald with huge eyebrows.

"Go away," said the old man. He sounded angry.

"Good morning," Ed said. "We are cleaning people's houses. We only charge five pounds. We vacuum and we mop and..."

"You go away before I call the police,"

shouted the old man and he slammed the door.

"You said people would be throwing
money at us. He looked like he wanted to
throw a brick at us!" said Zac.

"The next house will be better," said Ed.

"How do you know?" asked Zac.

"Because this time you are going to do the
talking," said Ed.

But the next house was no better. Or the one after that. Or the one after that. Everyone told them to go away and everyone threatened to call the police.

They came to the last house on Elm Road. They knocked on the door and waited. An old lady opened the door. She had put the chain on the door. Her long nose poked over the top of the chain.

"You leave me alone," she said in a shaky voice. "You better not try anything or I will call the police. I know what you want. Those girls told me all about you."

"Which girls?" asked Ed.

"The ones that cleaned my car," said the old lady. "They did a lovely job. That car has never been so clean and shiny."

Zac and Ed looked at the car outside the old lady's house. It was clean and shiny.

"What did these girls say?" asked Ed.

"They told me that two young thieves are going round the estate pretending to be cleaners. And that once they get inside your house they steal your money," said the old lady.

"You keep away from me," she said.

"Thieves?" said Zac.

"Steal money!" said Ed.

But before they could say anything else, the old lady shut her front door and bolted it.

"We are not thieves," called Ed through the letter box. "We are just cleaners!"

"You leave me alone or I will call the police," the old lady shouted back. "You should be ashamed of yourselves!"

"I can't believe Becca and Kat would tell people we were thieves," sighed Ed.

"It looks like they have been round the whole estate and told everyone!" said Zac.

"You know what this means, don't you," said Ed.

"It means we're not going snowboarding," said Zac.

"No," said Ed. "This means war!"

Chapter Five
The final challenge

That evening, Ed and Zac were up in Ed's room.

"I have a plan," said Ed.

"What is it?" asked Zac.

"Watch," said Ed.

Ed sent Kat a text.

You cheated. You told everyone we were thieves. We would have made loads more money than you if you hadn't cheated.

"What are you doing?" asked Zac.

"Wait," said Ed. His phone buzzed. Kat had replied. She had written,

We would have made more money than you anyway. We are going to win!

Ed laughed and typed a reply.

Really? Tomorrow, you do the house cleaning and we will do the car washing. You can borrow our vacuum cleaner and we will borrow your car cleaning stuff. And whoever makes the most money, gets to keep it. ALL of it. Is it a deal?

It wasn't long before Kat's reply came. It said,

OK. Meet outside your house at 10am. We can swap the vacuum cleaner and the car cleaning stuff.

"What are you doing?" cried Zac.

"They will end up with all our money!"

"We don't have any money," said Ed. "But we soon will!"

"How can you be so sure?" said Zac.

"Because," said Ed, "I have a plan."

That night, Ed sneaked out of bed and crept out into the garden. He went into the garden shed. Ten minutes later, he came back out of the shed with a vacuum cleaner. He left it by the front door and went back to bed.

Chapter Six
Showdown

The next morning, Zac and Ed were waiting for the girls outside Ed's house.

"Hang on a minute," said Zac, pointing at the vacuum cleaner. "That's not my mum's vacuum cleaner. Where did it come from?"

Ed began to laugh.

"It's my mum's old vacuum cleaner," he said.

"What's so funny about that?" asked Zac.

"You switch it on and it works for about two minutes. Then it just stops," Ed explained. "The girls won't make any money using it!"

Zac began to laugh too.

Kat and Becca arrived. The boys tried to stop laughing.

"We feel really bad about what happened yesterday," said Kat.

"It was really mean of you to tell everyone we were thieves," said Ed.

"We know," said Becca. "Sorry. So we thought we should make things right by calling the bet off. Why don't we share the money we made yesterday and all the money we make today. Is it a deal?"

Ed and Zac thought for a moment.

"Deal!" they said.

"But we are still doing the car washing," said Ed. "Is it a deal?"

Becca and Kat thought for a moment.

"Deal!" they said.

Becca and Kat handed the bucket, the sponge and the bottle of car shampoo to Ed and Zac.

Ed and Zac handed the vacuum cleaner and the bucket full of cleaning stuff over to Becca and Kat.

The girls looked up and down the road, chose a house and went and knocked on the front door. A smartly-dressed man opened the door. The boys watched as the man smiled and nodded and the girls dragged the vacuum cleaner into his house.

"You should have told them about the vacuum cleaner," said Zac.

"Wait until it stops working," laughed Ed. "It serves them right for what they did to us yesterday. We should stay here and see what happens!"

Chapter Seven
Oops!

The boys waited outside the house.

After a minute or two, they heard the sound of the vacuum cleaner starting up.

"How long did you say the vacuum cleaner works for?" asked Zac.

"About two minutes," said Ed, smiling. "And then it just stops."

Zac checked the time on his phone.

He began to laugh.

"The girls will think they have broken it," he said.

"Maybe we can get them to pay for it to be mended!" laughed Ed.

The boys listened.

"I can still hear it," said Zac. "Are you sure it will stop working?"

"Of course," said Ed. "It will stop any minute now."

Zac listened.

"The noise is getting louder," said Zac.

Ed listened. Zac was right.

"It sounds more like a racing car than a vacuum cleaner," said Zac.

"It sounds like a space rocket taking off!" said Ed.

"It sounds like..." But Zac did not have a chance to finish his sentence. He was interrupted by a loud explosion.

The door of the house flew open. A cloud of smoke billowed out of the door, followed by Kat, Becca and the smartly-dressed man. Except he didn't look so smart anymore. None of them did. They were covered from head to toe in dust.

Chapter Eight
Cleaning up again

Zac and Ed stared in horror at Becca and Kat and the smartly-dressed man. They were totally covered in dust and were coughing and spluttering.

"This is all **their** fault!" said Kat, pointing at Zac and Ed.

"They lent us the vacuum cleaner," said Becca.

"Right, you lot," said the man. "Get inside, right now!"

Zac, Ed, Becca and Kat all went into the man's living room.

Everything was covered in dust. Kat, Becca

and the man were all covered in dust. The vacuum cleaner stood smoking in the middle of the carpet.

The man looked like he might explode too. His face was bright red and he was making a strange puffing noise.

"Look what you have done!" he shouted. "Look what you have done to my house! My carpet! My sofa!"

"We're really sorry," said Becca.

"Really, really sorry," said Kat.

"Really, really, really sorry," said Ed.

"Very," added Zac.

"I'll have to get proper cleaners to tidy this mess up," said the man. "And you lot can pay for them"

Becca got out the money she and Kat had made the day before.

"Will this be enough?" she asked.

The man looked amazed.

"We washed cars all day yesterday to make some money," explained Kat. "We were trying to save up to pay for a school snowboarding trip to Scotland."

The man took the money. Ed, Zac, Kat and Becca walked out of the living room and into the hallway. They were about to leave when the man called them back.

"Here you are," he said.

The man handed Kat back one of the twenty pound notes.

"It won't pay for a snowboarding trip," said the man. "But it should pay for the four of you to go down to the ice rink to go skating this afternoon – after you've helped me tidy up."

Becca and Kat and Ed and Zac thought for a moment.

"Snowboarding is very dangerous," said Becca.

"You could break your leg," said Kat.

"Or fall off a mountain," added Ed.

"Ice skating would be much safer," said Zac.

"And we'd have money left for a bag of chips to share," said Kat, looking at the twenty pound note in her hand.

"Is it a deal?" said the man.

"Deal!" said Kat, Becca, Ed and Zac all at once.

Bonus Bits!
David Grant

Have you ever thought about becoming an author? Here are some fascinating and surprising facts about the author of this book.

David Grant was born in London.

He was an English teacher for 12 years – he taught lots of stroppy teenagers!

Before he was a teacher he was the manager of a record shop.

He now has 3 children, 3 dogs, 2 geese and 7 chickens and lives in Wales.

David writes plays as well as stories.

He has now given up teaching to write his books full time and look after his children and animals!

Test your knowledge

Turn to the back for the answers (no peeking along the way!)

1. Why did Zac read the letters he got from school?

a)   he liked to know what was happening

b)   his mum had told him off before when she had found 20 letters in his bag

c)   he had written them himself

2. What are Ed, Zac, Becca and Kat trying to earn money for?

a)   a museum visit

b)   a camping trip

c)   a skiing and snowboarding trip

3. What did Zac's mum want in return for the boys borrowing the vacuum cleaner?

a)   her house cleaned for free

b)   half the money they earned

c)   her car cleaned for free

4. Whose bucket, sponge and shampoo did the girls borrow?

a)   Becca's dad

b)   Kat's dad

c)   Ed's dad

5. Why did people not want Ed and Zac to clean their houses?

a)   they did not do a good job

b)   they had a broken vacuum cleaner

c)   the girls said they were thieves

6. What did Ed think would happen to the vacuum cleaner he lent the girls?

a)   it would stop working after 2 minutes

b)   it would explode

c)   it would not work at all

7. What deal did the children make with the man at the end of the story?

a)   clean up his house for free

b)   clean up his house for £20

c)   give him all the money to clean up his house

Guess who?

Read each piece of information below and decide whether it is about Ed, Zac, Becca or Kat.

A. Never reads letters from school.

B. Came up with the idea to clean cars.

C. Came up with the idea to clean houses.

D. Tells the man that it is Zac and Ed's fault.

What do you think?

Were the girls were right to tell people that the boys were thieves? Why?

Were the boys were right to give the girls a faulty vacuum cleaner?

Were the children right to give up on their dream of going on the trip?

What next?

Imagine the boys earned £200 and the girls had earned £200. They would have had enough money for one girl and one boy to go on the trip. What do you think they might have done? How could they resolve this? Why not write an extra chapter for the book about what might have happened.

Answers to 'test your knowledge'

1. b) His mum had told him off before when she had found 20 letters in his bag

2. c) a skiing and snowboarding trip

3. a) her house cleaned for free

4. a) Becca's dad

5. c) the girls said they were thieves

6. a) it would stop working after 2 minutes

7. b) clean up his house for £20